C000121667

Bookclub-in-a-Box presents the discussion companion for Alice Sebold's novel

The Lovely Bones

Published by Little, Brown and Company. Boston, 2002.
ISBN: 0-316-66634-3

Quotations used in this guide have been taken from the text of the hardcover edition of **The Lovely Bones**. All information taken from other sources is acknowledged.

This discussion companion for **The Lovely Bones** has been prepared and written by Marilyn Herbert, originator of Bookclub-in-a-Box. Marilyn Herbert. B.Ed., is a teacher, librarian, speaker and writer. Bookclub-in-a-Box is a unique guide to current fiction and classic literature intended for book club discussions, educational study seminars, and personal pleasure. For more information about the Bookclub-in-a-Box team, visit our website.

Bookclub-in-a-Box discussion companion for The Lovely Bones

ISBN 10: 0-9733984-8-5
ISBN 13: 9780973398489

This guide reflects the perspective of the Bookclub-in-a-Box team and is the sole property of Bookclub-in-a-Box.

CONTACT INFORMATION: SEE BACK COVER.

BOOKCLUB-IN-A-BOX

Alice Sebold's The Lovely Bones

BOOKCLUB-IN-A-BOX

Readers and Leaders Guide

Each Bookclub-in-a-Box guide is clearly and effectively organized to give you information and ideas for a lively discussion, as well as to present the major highlights of the novel. The format, with a Table of Contents, allows you to pick and choose the specific points you wish to talk about. It does not have to be used in any prescribed order. In fact, it is meant to support, not determine, your discussion.

You Choose What to Use.

You may find that some information is repeated in more than one section and may be cross-referenced so as to provide insight on the same idea from different angles.

The guide is formatted to give you extra space to make your own notes.

How to Begin

Relax and look forward to enjoying your bookclub.

With Bookclub-in-a-Box as your behind the scenes support, there is little for you to do in the way of preparation.

Some readers like to review the guide after reading the novel; some before. Either way, the guide is all you will need as a companion for your discussion. You may find that the guide's interpretation, information, and background have sparked other ideas not included.

Having read the novel and armed with Bookclub-in-a-Box, you will be well prepared to lead or guide or listen to the discussion at hand.

Lastly, if you need some more 'hands-on' support, feel free to contact us. (See Contact Information)

What to Look For

Each Bookclub-in-a-Box guide is divided into easy-to-use sections, which include points on characters, themes, writing style and structure, literary or historical background, author information, and other pertinent features unique to the novel being discussed. These may vary slightly from guide to guide.

INTERPRETATION OF EACH NOVEL REFLECTS THE PERSPECTIVE OF THE
BOOKCLUB-IN-A-BOX TEAM.

Do We Need to Agree?
THE ANSWER TO THIS QUESTION IS NO.

If we have sparked a discussion or a debate on certain points, then we are
happy. We invite you to share your group's alternative findings and experiences with us. You can respond on-line at our website or contact us through
our Contact Information. We would love to hear from you.

Discussion Starters

There are as many ways to begin a bookclub discussion as there are members in your group. If you are an experienced group, you will already have
your favorite ways to begin. If you are a newly formed group or a group
looking for new ideas, here are some suggestions.

Ask for people's impressions of the novel. (This will give you some idea
about which parts of the unit to focus on.)

- Identify a favorite or major character.

- Identify a favorite or major idea.

- Begin with a powerful or pertinent quote. (not necessarily from the
  novel)

- Discuss the historical information of the novel. (not applicable to all
  novels)

- If this author is familiar to the group, discuss the range of his/her
  work and where this novel stands in that range.

- Use the discussion topics and questions in the bookclub-in-a-box
  guide.

If you have further suggestions for discussion starters, be sure to share
them with us and we will share them with others.

Above All, Enjoy Yourselves

INTRODUCTION

Suggested Beginnings

Novel Quickline

Key to the Novel

Author Information

INTRODUCTION

Suggested Beginnings

1. The Lovely Bones seems to fit in the genre of magical realism, but in reality it is more like imaginative realism. The story has elements that lie just outside the certainty of our experience.

How does this affect your response to the story?

2. The novel appears to be structured as a murder mystery but does not focus on Susie's murder. Instead, it concentrates on the effects the murder has on others.

Does this technique successfully relate to the telling of the story? Is the reader prepared?

3. The five stages of grief according to Elisabeth Kübler-Ross's book, *On Death and Dying*, are the following: denial and isolation, anger, bargaining, depression, and acceptance.

Compare these five stages of grieving to the grieving process that Susie's loved ones go through in the novel. (see Central Premise, p.27)

4. The novel is filled with clichés and simplified language.

What is it about these common expressions that appeals to readers? Is this writing style effective? Why is it used?

5. T.S. Eliot said, *"It is worth dying to find out what life is."*

Connect this thought to the novel.

Novel Quickline

Susie Salmon is fourteen when she is murdered. In the realm of our experience, this should mean that Susie has tragically disappeared and can no longer be in contact with anyone. But this is not the world according to Susie or Sebold. Their world is one of imaginative realism, where Susie tells us her story from heaven.

We watch Susie and listen as she makes the transition from her earthly life to her heavenly one. With Susie, we observe how her family copes with the horrific loss of a child. We observe the very common stages of grief that they necessarily experience, and like Susie, we wait to see if they successfully transcend this experience and are able to continue with the job of living.

What is different about the story told in **The Lovely Bones** is that Susie herself must go through this transition. She is in the inbetween, no longer on Earth, but not yet in her final heaven. Sebold takes everyone, Susie and her family, through a maturation process. She especially includes the reader, who is not allowed the luxury of detached observation. We must join the Salmon family on their emotional journey.

Susie is forever "trapped in a perfect world", but it's nice to know that even a perfect world can change and grow.

Key to the Novel

Imaginative Realism

- As readers, we are more familiar with the concept of magical realism through the work of writers like Gabriel Garcia Marquez (**One Hundred Years of Solitude**), John Fowles (**The Magus**), Gina Nahai (**Moonlight on the Avenue of Faith**), Lilian Nattel (**The River Midnight**). In order to be classified as magical realism, a story must include magical elements for both the characters and the plot. For example, people would be able to fly; there would be outside influences and unnatural forces that help to create a magical environment.

- Imaginative realism, a process used by painters in the 1920s, differs from magical realism by its focus on the re-imagining or re-positioning of real things.

- Both imagination and magic rely on the suspension of disbelief. The imaginative process focuses on the true nature of things, whereas the magical process relies on the unnatural.

notes

Author Information

- Alice Sebold was born in 1963 in Madison, Wisconsin, and was raised in Philadelphia. She is married to successful writer Glen David Gold, author of **Carter Beats the Devil.** They live in Long Beach, California.

- Sebold entered the B.A. program at the University of Syracuse but did not complete it. She finally obtained her B.A. in English at the University of Houston and later received her M.F.A. in fiction at the University of California, Irvine.

- In her freshman year, she was the victim of a random rape attack. As a result, she dropped out of school and moved to New York, where she spent years in low-level jobs (including some teaching and restaurant work), bad relationships, and some experimentation with drugs and alcohol. About six months after the attack, she was traumatically confronted by her rapist in a chance street encounter, when he casually asked if he knew her from somewhere.

- Between academic degrees, Sebold worked as a caretaker in an arts colony, where the inhabitants lived on and from the land. She credits this electricity-free situation with helping to ground her life.

- Sebold maintains that she had always wanted to be a writer and includes in her checkered career the accomplishment of having written for the *New York Times* and the *Chicago Tribune.* New York's *The Village Voice* named her a "Writer on the Verge".

- Prior to the publication of her memoir, **Lucky,** and **The Lovely Bones,** Sebold wrote three other novels, none of which were published. When Sebold began the writing of what was to be **The Lovely Bones,** she quickly realized that her personal issues were getting in the way. Not wanting **The Lovely Bones** to be an autobiographical, self-healing type of novel, she stopped and began her memoir, **Lucky.**

notes

- The title to her memoir comes from a casual police comment that, as a victim, Sebold was one of the lucky ones. Another victim, attacked at the same spot, had been murdered and dismembered. Sebold's memoir tells the whole tale of her incident, including the arrest and trial of her attacker.

- An incidence of violence, either experienced personally or by someone close, is a life-altering experience, which can often disturb and alienate the victim and his/her loved ones. Sebold's goal in writing the novel was to take the "alienation" out of the alienating experience. She uses her fiction as a type of sensitivity training.

  > *I had an experience close to being killed, and of course that naturally makes me think of those people who were, and feel some connection to them in that way ... I think I'm fascinated by the connections between the living and the dead, and I'm also very compelled by the sense of alienation that people feel who have experienced violence, both victims themselves and the family members of those victims. And so I'm certainly driven by a will to lessen that alienation.* (The Globe and Mail, July 13, 2002)

- In another interview, Sebold says, *"It wasn't my dream to grow up, get raped and write a book about it ... I always dreamed of being a novelist."* But as Abigail observes in the novel, goals can get sidetracked. When that happens, choices must be made. Sebold made the choice to use fiction to reach out to others through her own experiences.

- Sebold's primary goal with **The Lovely Bones** is to help normalize grief and take the discussion of it into a comfortable realm in daily life. Often we try to protect those grieving by wrapping them in isolation. We do this because we are lost as to what else to say to them. Sebold tells the grieving: Come in and be with me.

- Ruth is the character in the novel most closely modeled after Sebold. Like Ruth, Sebold always considered herself to have odd reactions and observations to things and people. Ever since she was small, Sebold thought herself to be a bit weird. She writes poetry, not for publication, but for her own personal comfort and growth. As a writer, Sebold is determined and focused. Her routine is to get up between 3 and 5 am and work until noon. She likes writing when it's dark and quiet, a fact she incorporates into her novel, using many descriptively dark images.

Bibliographic Information

- **Lucky,** (1999)

- **The Lovely Bones** (2002) - has sold over a million copies. It became a sleeper hit and an overnight success.

- Film rights have been purchased by British filmmaker Lynne Ramsay (*Ratcatcher*).

- American reviewers were mostly enthusiastic about the book but carried a common theme: If they had known what the book was about, they would never have read it. British reviews have been more cautious and critical of the narrative techniques in the novel, but it is beginning to do well both there and in Australia.

CHARACTERIZATION

Names

CHARACTERIZATION

Sebold has drawn characters that remain simple and consistent within the context of the novel's situation: the murder of a child. Sebold does not stray far from the scene of the crime.

There are few extraneous descriptions or explanations because this book is not about the psychology of the characters but about how one deals with grief.

- For instance, there is little discussion of Abigail's complex and emotional relationship with her mother, Lynn. It is enough to know that Abigail had suffered a loss previous to Susie's murder: her father first left her, and then he died.

- Nor is there an over-emphasis on George Harvey's misguided and abusive childhood. We don't need to understand his multiple, psychological deficiencies. Sebold only sketches enough information to address the question of why he murders.

Sebold skillfully takes her characters deep within themselves, into the dark of self-alienation, before bringing them back up into the light. (See Dark to Light, p.51) Each character must come to the realization that strength comes from mutual protection, not from isolation.

Names

Sebold has chosen strong, plain names so that the personality of each character is reflected in the number of syllables in each name.

- One syllable: Jack, Ruth, Ray, Lynn, and Len are characters who are straightforward and openly committed to their beliefs. There are no twists or turns to their personalities.

- Two syllables: Susie, Harvey, Lindsey, and Buckley are more complicated characters because they experience two-sided and sometimes contradictory emotions. With the exception of George Harvey, each individual goes through a process of growth. Each of Harvey's other victims also have two-syllable names: Jackie, Leah, Sophie, Wendy.

- Three syllables: Abigail and Ruana have the furthest to go in accepting their lot in life and in growing through their respective grief. Abigail is by far a more important character in the novel, and we see her progress most clearly. However, we see glimpses of Ruana's concerns and struggles as well.

Susie Salmon

- Susie is a typical fourteen-year-old, who considers herself both innocent and curious. This curiosity leads her to experiment with the world and ultimately costs her life.

- The Salmon name is emphasized twice and is an interesting image. *"My name is Susie, last name Salmon, like the fish."* (p.5 & p.309) A salmon's mission in life is to swim upstream against all obstacles and odds in order to recreate itself by laying new eggs. Sebold uses this image to show us that life's possibilities don't necessarily flow in an obvious manner. Life can work against gravity; Susie reaches us from heaven in order to enlighten us about the life-and-death process. She encourages us to travel upstream to work against any preconceived notions of life and death.

- Susie's dream on earth was to be a wildlife photographer. Ironically, the wildlife she observes from heaven is the human kind.

Jack Salmon

- Jack, Susie's father, has a difficult time with Susie's death. Through Jack, we see fear, withdrawal, and isolation. Jack is afraid all the time. He's hard on Lindsey and Buckley because he fears losing another child.

- He retreats into his house and into his memories because he cannot face the people around him who act *"as if having a dead child were contagious."* (p.159) Jack, as his name indicates, is single-minded in his grief.

- Eventually he grows into the realization that he can care *"for his two daughters by caring for one [Lindsey]."* (p.162) However, his relationship with Buckley remains a bit more complicated.

notes

Abigail Salmon

- Of all the characters in the book, with the exception of Susie, it is Abigail, Susie's mother, who we get to know in more detail. The reason for this highlights the fragility, strength, and complexity of the mother-child bond. We learn a bit about Abigail's relationship with her own father and mother, her hopes and dreams, her emotions and behavior.

- Jack calls her Ocean Eyes because, as he says, they are eyes to get lost in. Len Fenerman also drowns in the look of Abigail's eyes. They are impossible to read because there are no landmarks; the water is deep and wide and indecipherable. Abigail keeps much to herself. As a child, Susie observed her mother and sees *"how the life she had wanted and the loss of it reached her in waves."* (p.149)

- With some regret, Abigail gave up an academic life for that of marriage and motherhood. Susie captures this look of regret in her photograph of Abigail, (p.43) which shows clearly how Abigail lays her grief over Susie on top of all her other griefs.

  > *... she had been punished in the most horrible and unimaginable way for never having wanted me.*
  > (Susie, p.266)

- Abigail's troubled relationship with her own mother, Lynn, stems from Lynn's relationship with her husband, a philanderer who never justified his actions or made excuses. Abigail is dealing with a double loss: her father and her daughter.

Ruth

- Ruth is the character closest to representing Alice Sebold. Ruth is the intense writer, the "weird" one with few close personal ties. Her life changed in the instant that Susie brushed past her on her way from earth. She was touched by this angel.

- With few friends, Ruth's *"journal was her closest and most important relationship."* (p.252) Through the journal, we get a glimpse of another life, one that brings Ruth in touch with the spiritual side of herself and others. **The Lovely Bones** is Ruth's (Sebold's) journal.

George Harvey

- To say that George Harvey is strange is an understatement. Even the neighbors describe him as a *"character"*. (p.10) Through Susie's eyes, we see Harvey as lonely, unmarried, someone who eats frozen meals for dinner, and doesn't own a pet. Susie, the child, sees him as a stereotype, an "everyman" who is granted sympathy from a distance.

- There are no records anywhere of a George Harvey, as he is known in Susie's town. Officially, Harvey does not exist; physically, Susie no longer exists. There is no body, only a single bone.

- While Sebold does not go into a psychological analysis of George Harvey's character, she allows us a glimpse into his perspective. Harvey knows how to look past the dead because his mother taught him that sometimes there are *"good trinkets to take away from them."* (p.188) Trinkets to have and to count. (see Counting, p.49)

- Harvey does not need to be in heaven to see how life should be lived. He knows that the worst things to be are a child or a woman. He knows because he has caused harm to both.

notes

- It is not until too late that proof of Harvey's guilt is found on a coke bottle where his fingerprints appear beside Susie's. (p.218)

Lindsey

- Lindsey, the remaining Salmon sister, exemplifies the strategies needed when coping with grief. She is the most logical choice for this because all the other characters are either too young or too damaged to demonstrate what Sebold is offering as grief counsel.

- We watch Lindsey as she learns how to breathe, how she shuts down her heart to protect herself (p.32, 34), but how she allows Samuel to help her heal. Throughout the novel, Lindsey continually climbs from the dark to the light.

- She is the sister who is a visible reminder of what Susie might have been had she lived. Susie is very happy to see that Lindsey succeeds in surviving her grief. It is Susie who uses the birth of Lindsey's first child to let go of the family. (see Letting Go, p.34)

Buckley

- Buckley is a casualty of the grief over Susie's death. He is only four years old at the time and has to grow and mature in the shadow of the sister who is no longer in the picture.

- He suffers the most, because he has no one to help him interpret Susie's death. Everyone is so busy dealing with their own grief, they overlook his.

- It is his picture, however, his drawing of heaven and earth, that gives the novel its unique perspective on life and death.

Hours before I died, my mother hung on the refrigerator a picture that Buckley had drawn. In the drawing a thick blue line separated the air and ground. In the days that followed I watched my family walk back and forth past that drawing and I became convinced that that blue line was a real place – an Inbetween, where heaven's horizon met Earth's. I wanted to go there into the cornflower blue of Crayola, the royal, the turquoise, the sky. (p.34)

- As a child, Buckley is the most capable of crossing the line between imagination and reality. What child hasn't had an imaginary friend? As adults, we accept the child's easy transition between what is real and what is imagined. Through the novel, we see when Buckley "sees" Susie. Buckley brings us the possibility of Susie's "Inbetween" and the possibility of the transparent veil that hides the departed but may not completely conceal them.

Detective Len Fenerman

Detective Len serves a number of purposes:

- First, and most obviously, he is part of the framework of the murder-mystery. A crime is committed. The police are dispatched to search out and piece together the clues. But clues are not always obvious and can be obscured by normal human reactions. In complying with the statement of justice that declares a person innocent until proven guilty, the detective is exasperated by Jack's obsessive and intuitive assertion that Harvey is guilty of Susie's death. Len orders Jack to stop hounding Harvey. In the face of Jack's angry grief, Harvey seems all the more reasonable.

> *[Harvey] had an explanation that fit so perfectly, they did not see him as a flight risk - largely because they did not see him first and foremost as a murderer.* (p.192)

- Secondly, Fenerman reinforces the fact that, as much as everyone would like them neatly wrapped up, many crimes remain unsolved. The detective keeps photos of the victims of his unsolved crimes and continually counts them. (see Counting, p.49)

- Thirdly, Len is a reflection of Abigail's bottomless grief and, at the same time, offers her a release from it. Susie watches them.

> *I felt the kisses as they came down my mother's neck and onto her chest, like the small, light feet of mice, and like the flower petals falling that they were. Ruinous and marvelous all at once. They were whispers calling her away from me and from her family and from her grief. She followed with her body.* (p.196)

Grandma Lynn

- Susie's grandmother is a unique character, one who drags the light back into the darkness of the house. She is flamboyant, irritatingly cheerful, a drinker, a flirt; in other words, she is the complete opposite of her daughter, Abigail.

- We only find out later that Lynn's life with her adulterous husband was a difficult one. Despite this, she has no apologies or regrets except one: Lynn is saddened by her relationship with her daughter.

- As an elder in the novel's cast of characters, Lynn concludes that life offers few choices. She must quietly come to terms with Abigail's escape from home in the same way she had to accept her husband's long-ago abandonment and just as she must now accept Susie's death. She is realistically determined to move forward.

*[Lynn] no longer believed in talk. It never rescued any-
thing. At seventy she had come to believe in time alone.*
(p.254)

Hal and Samuel

- Hal and Samuel Heckler are the pair of brothers that offset the
  Salmon sisters. Hal is a compassionate and very useful friend to the
  family. He is always available when needed.

- Samuel turns out to be the love of Lindsey's life. Their relationship
  juxtaposes the horror of Susie's circumstances and death.

  *At fourteen, my sister sailed away from me into a place
  I'd never been. In the walls of my sex there was horror and blood, in the walls of hers there were windows.*
  (p.125)

- Sebold presents the sisters at the same age but on opposite sides of
  the sexual experience, just as the sisters are now on opposite sides of
  living.

- Samuel is *"the fixer of broken things"*, **(p.237)** and he helps fix
  Lindsey and the family. He brings more light to the darkness of the
  house. **(see Dark to Light, p.51)**

FOCUS POINTS & THEMES

Central Premise

Belief/Disbelief

Brokenness

Connections

Transition/Transcendence

Letting Go

FOCUS POINTS AND THEMES

Central Premise

The primary themes of the novel are learning to live with loss and learning to begin to let go. These themes are parallel and not opposite. Sebold addresses these issues from both sides of the dividing line of life and shows that everyone, living and dead, has a job to do.

- First, it is the goal of those left behind to let go of their loss; only then can the dead truly find peace and rest.

- Second, Sebold adds the message that the dead also need to let go. It is only then that they can leave what Sebold refers to as the "Inbetween" and move to their permanent heaven.

The ultimate goal for everyone is to find peace at the end of the grieving process.

This premise is built on a series of five ideas that parallel the grief process as outlined by psychologist Elisabeth Kübler-Ross. (Backer)

Sebold	Kübler-Ross
• Belief/Disbelief	• Denial/Isolation
• Brokenness	• Anger
• Transition/Transcendence	• Bargaining
• Connections	• Depression
• Letting Go	• Acceptance

Belief / Disbelief *(Denial/Isolation)*

- The novel's individual characters go through the process of believing or not believing the idea of life outside of death, each to a varying degree. Each must first accept Susie's death, and then each must choose or reject the possibility of something existing on the other side of life. This does not end up as a denial of death but becomes a place where ultimate comfort can be found.

- Through her use of common and familiar images and experiences, Sebold challenges the reader, as well as her characters, to look differently at this changed image of death. She appeals to our knowledge of countless, extraordinary and unbelievable survival stories found in religious texts and/or in newspaper accounts of cats and children falling from great heights. (p.303)

- As further support, Sebold presents the universal experience of pregnant women, who experience the presence of life in the subtle flutter of the fetus. This illustrates the possibility of how the presence of the dead can be felt. (p.323)

- The night that Susie died, Ruth immediately believed that she was touched by Susie leaving the earth. She knew she had to write about it and became open to the possibility that the dead do interact with the living in many ways. (p.36, 325)

- Even Ray is an example of someone who chooses to use blind faith in order to believe something. As a doctor, he understands that he may be presented with medical situations and possibilities that cannot always be accounted for through logical reasoning. Ray knows he needs to choose what to believe or disbelieve in order to best serve his patients. (p.325)

- Sebold continually presents situations in which choice must be made between believing and not believing. She continues to stack the deck by piling the incidents one on top of the other until she arrives at the climactic scene between Ruth/Susie and Ray. We are then confronted with the possibility that Susie has truly entered Ruth's body.

- The message is simple, reader: Believe or don't believe, but make the choice.

Brokenness   *(Anger)*

- Susie's death has broken each character in the novel. Each experiences anger but is unable to share the pain of this anger. Susie's parents had never found themselves *"broken together."* (p.20) Their familiar response was for one to remain strong while the other needed support. But this time, both parents are broken.

- For Jack, the image of brokenness is physical – he smashes the ships in the bottles and has his knee broken by a baseball bat. For Abigail, it is the moment she is confronted with Susie's hat: *"something broke in [Abigail]. The fine wall of leaden crystal that had protected her heart ... shattered."* (p.28)

- Sebold once talked about all experiences being beautiful, even if that beauty is about "brokenness". In this way she models herself after such writers as Tolstoy and Marquez, both of whom write about people and relationships that are broken.

- With this approach, Sebold feels free to take her story in any direction, and, she therefore chooses to break through the stage of anger by exploring the beauty of heaven after life on earth is broken.

- She concentrates on how to mend shattered relationships by beginning new ones: Lindsey and Samuel are a new couple making a fresh start. Through Samuel, the *"fixer of broken things"*, (p.237) Sebold shows there is hope in accepting the brokenness of things.

Connections *(Bargaining – Trading, Joining)*

- Sebold uses the central symbol of bones to show connections between things and people. The only part of Susie ever found is the elbow bone, a joint connecting two sections of the arm. Jack's knee is a similar joining bone. Like bones, relationships and other connections are made, broken, rejoined, or maintained throughout the novel. Connections, or the lack of connections, are the tools that the living use to navigate their grief.

- In contrast to the solid individual connections that her characters make, Sebold presents the connection between heaven and earth as transparent. Together with the characters, we, the readers, are asked

to become open to the alternative idea that a connection to the other side might be possible. Sebold talks about "break-through", a point at which Susie is seen by people on earth. The first time she breaks through the barrier between life and death is by accident. She finds her father talking to her, while he is looking at the model boats in a bottle they made together.

> *I watched him as he lined up the ships in bottles on his desk ... there was the one that had burst into flames in the week before my death.*
>
> *He smashed that one first.*
>
> *... It was then that, without knowing how, I revealed myself. In every piece of glass, in every shard and sliver, I cast my face.* (p.46)

- Whether people see her in their mind's eye or in actual reflection, these "break-through" moments represent Susie's connection to the family after her death. Everyone sees Susie at some point, most especially Buckley, who sees her image in the mirror. The reader is reminded immediately of Lewis Carroll's classic tale, **Through the Looking Glass**. Sebold reminds us that if we look carefully, we might also see that the mirror is transparent.

- Susie makes her final and most lasting connection to the reader through her story. She wants us to know *"... the story of [her] family. Because horror on Earth is real and it is every day. It is like a flower or like the sun; it cannot be contained."* (p.186)

- The story itself must be spread like nature, like sunlight, with the goal of connecting to the reader. Confirming these connections allows even the dead victims to move on. We hear from Susie and Flora:

Our heartache poured into one another like water from cup to cup. Each time I told my story, I lost a bit, the smallest drop of pain. (p.186)

Transition / Transcendence   *(Depression)*

- Transition is the move or change from one state or condition to another, whereas transcendence is the move into a completely new state of being, possibly one that is beyond the range of human experience. The state of grief, which follows a shock, can thus become a different, yet familiar emotion that overpowers all else. Grief can be a transition stage or a state in which one remains.

- Sebold has her characters represent transition by constantly moving them from the dark into the light. As well, she uses the sink-hole as a symbol for sinking into depression. The novel's characters must fight darkness and depression in order to transcend them. (see Symbols, p.49)

- Changes and transitions of all kinds take place in the story: plans change, goals change, people change, life changes. The goal in life is to be open to change and work with it. When a person cannot transcend, that person can become frozen or trapped. Sebold uses the images of the snow globe, the ships inside glass bottles, and photographs to represent this state of being. She introduces us to the familiar concept of the living dead, wounded people who have let go of life even while they are living it. Ray's father is described as a living ghost, trapped in his marriage.

  He walked in the room like a ghost and like a ghost slipped in between the sheets, barely creasing them.
  (p.314)

- Sebold's most obvious image of transition/transcendence is Susie's transit from earth to heaven. Before she was killed, she experiences a powerful moment common to victims of rape. *"I began to leave my body; I began to inhabit the air and the silence."* (p.14)

- Again, Sebold uses familiar imagery to illustrate the possible transition between heaven and earth.

  > *I remembered once, with my parents and Lindsey and Buckley, riding backward on a train into a dark tunnel. That was how it felt to leave Earth the second time. The destination somehow inevitable, the sights seen in passing so many times ... I knew we were taking a long trip to a place very far away.* (p.311)

- Change/transition is further emphasized with the idea of boundary lines being invisible or as having the edges fuzzy and indistinct. When Susie sees Harvey later in the book, *"the edges of Mr. Harvey seemed oddly blurred ... "* (p.291)

- Not all transitions are positive. Buckley's open innocence at the age of four ends with a hardening of his heart at age fourteen. He can't reach beyond.

  > *Deep inside ... this four-year-old sat, his heart flashing. Heart to stone, heart to stone.* (p.269)

- Other transitions take the form of escape. Abigail escapes twice: once into Detective Fenerman's arms, the second time to California. Mr. Harvey escapes from town just at the moment that he was likely to be arrested.

- Plans change; goals change. Transitions become the new goal.

Letting Go   *(acceptance)*

- Letting go is the ultimate goal of both the living and the dead by laying grief to rest and allowing existence to continue on both sides of the veil. If this is successfully accomplished, there would be no grieving souls, who are like the living-dead and there would be no restless souls disturbing the air around us.

- Letting go is a deliberate choice and implies moving forward without being burdened by grief. Buckley forces his father to choose between him, the living child, and Susie, the dead child. **(p.256)** Susie herself eventually must make the choice between staying in limbo on earth, or going to heaven permanently.

  > *I was almost blinded by ... this choice; the idea that if I'd remained on Earth I could have left this place to claim another, that I could go anywhere I wanted to. And I wondered then, was it the same in heaven as on Earth? What I'd been missing was a wanderlust that came from letting go?* **(p.305)**

- The key to letting go is acceptance. Abigail has the hardest time because she has the most to let go: Her grief contains her mother, father, and daughter. But in the end, she does open herself to the possibility of letting go, and we begin to sense that she will eventually find it easier to face the possibility of a future.

- The best and most convincing image of resolving grief and letting go occurs when Lindsey names her baby Abigail Suzanne. The baby's first name is for Abigail, the living mother/grandmother; the second name is for the remembrance of Susie, the deceased sister/aunt. Susie is finally *"left ... in ... memories, where [she is] meant to be."* **(p.327)** The concept of using names to create a living memory of a loved one is found in many cultures.

WRITING STRUCTURE

Perfect Murder

Setting

Title

Narration

WRITING STRUCTURE

Sebold structures the novel around the murder of Susie Salmon. The murder opens the story but is quickly moved out of the way. Although it is the frame for the story, it is not the focus of Sebold's exploration. However, it is the perfect murder.

- We must look at the murder and at the rest of the story within the context of two perceptions: to see things that are possible and to see things that are plausible. The difference in meaning between these two ideas forms the basis of Sebold's premise and her themes.

- The story of the murder must be logistically possible in order to be convincing. Just reading the daily newspaper in recent years is proof positive that a murder, like Susie's, is possible.

- Sebold then offers forth the idea that Susie's reaching out from beyond the grave is plausible. The story of Susie's heaven may not be found within the realm of our experience or our imagination, but Sebold argues in favor of such a heaven and presents it as a plausibility; that is, as a situation that may not be proved by facts, but one that may likely be true even without proof. In other words, if something is both chronologically logical (as in a possible sequence of events) and emotionally convincing (as in the stages of grieving), then the situation is one that can likely be believed.

- Therefore, Susie's story can be considered plausible. The concept of Susie's talking to us from heaven may not be able to be proved but the reverse is also true: it cannot be proved that it can't or hasn't happened.

Perfect Murder

- Sebold's novel is a creative play on the category of mystery writing. The mystery genre is established twice: in a show of equal opportunity, both Harvey and Susie commit the perfect crime, and they both, literally, get away with murder.

- Susie's murder is quite real. In real life, there are many unsolved crimes, such as those illustrated by Detective Len's photograph collection. Unfortunately there are too many horrific real-life examples, all of which are possible.

- Susie's crime originates with a school contest, where the challenge is to develop the perfect murder weapon. The icicle is that perfect weapon because it disappears by melting. In a twist of imaginative revenge, the icicle knocks Harvey into a deep, snow-covered ravine, where he is left to die. This situation parallels the fate of Harvey's victims, many of whom were never found or were found much too late. These situations make perfect sense and therefore are plausible.

Setting

- The story takes place in the 1970s, a time of innocence, when events like Susie's murder were relatively rare and still shocking. Significantly, it is also a time before the availability of DNA testing. If this story were set today, this would be a very short novel.

- The epigraph to the novel is from a passage in the story in which Susie's father describes the penguin's life inside the snow globe. *"Don't worry, Susie; he has a nice life. He's trapped in a perfect world."* It is this snow globe image that Sebold uses as the setting for Susie's heaven: it is pleasantly calm and transparent but is a very separate space.

- When Susie holds the globe in real life, this is a familiar situation to all of us; when Susie, in heaven, holds the globe of life, it becomes a symbolic situation. In the course of Sebold's story, Susie is not fully inside either globe.

- Sebold takes this same image to another level and shows how it can become an image of entrapment, where hell and hope are caught in the same snare. When Detective Len arrives to return the Pennsylvania keystone charm from Susie's bracelet, Susie's parents are afraid to hear that Susie's body had also been found. They react *"... like animals trapped in ice – their eyes frozen open beseeching whoever walked above them to release them now, please."* (p.290)

Title

- The title, **The Lovely Bones**, is the novel's main symbol and metaphor for the idea of connections. Bones form a skeleton, which is covered by skin. This book is about the "bare bones" of the grief process, which is overlaid with detail and humor, both of which give the book its meaning and purpose.

... lovely bones ... had grown around my absence ... I began to see things in a way that let me hold the world without me in it. The events that my death wrought were merely the bones of a body that would become whole at some unpredictable time in the future. The price of what I came to see as this miraculous body had been my life. **(p.320)**

- Once again there is a cross-reference to a transparent globe.

Narration

- Susie is the omniscient observer, the narrator from heaven. From her vantage point, she sees all. Despite this clear advantage, Susie's biased emotions do come through. It is her age-appropriate language and emotional range that makes her existence plausible and believable. She is bewildered, frightened, confused, disappointed, generous, joyful, and caring; she shows a predictable age-related innocence about people and the ways of the world. For example, she understands and accepts Ruth, whom she doesn't know well, while her close friend, Clarissa, disappoints her.

- Even though she is in heaven, Susie still grows and matures. This strengthens Sebold's point that maturity is not only related to chronological age, but to experience. Susie grows even after death. Because Susie weaves her story in and out of the family's life, both before and after death, we see that there were cracks in the family unit all along, and we see how her death widened those cracks.

notes

- Susie's growth process in heaven parallels the grief process on earth. The cracks can be filled through the full process of grief growth; death should not be an absolute end. Sebold confirms that the dead can continue to exert an influence on all loved ones, hopefully in a positive way. It is up to us to choose whether or not to believe that.

WRITING STYLE

Language

WRITING STYLE

Language

- Sebold's choice of language is based on simplicity and innocence. Her dialogue, images, and explanations are carefully placed inside common down-to-earth words and phrases. They are effective, vivid, and consistent in tone. After Abigail returned, Lindsey had to call her mother "Mom". *"It tasted soapy and foreign in her mouth."* **(p.267)** Washing out a child's mouth with soap was once a common parental chastisement.

- There is a lot of easygoing teenage humor, especially from Susie. Although she is unhappy to watch everyone suffering, she knows she is all right and has relaxed up to a point where she feels bad to know that folks are starting to move on. Like many typical teens, she is focused on herself.

Where was I? Would I be mentioned? Brought up and discussed? Usually now the answer was a disappointing no. It was no longer a Susie-fest on Earth. (p.236)

- Sebold's sparse sentences are deadly in their accuracy. When Abigail arrives in California, she first walks along the beach looking out into the endless horizon (another metaphor for heaven). She comes across a baby on a beach. *"New fresh infant girls to replace your own? As my mother laughed and I watched her face light up, I also saw it fall into strange lines."* (p.223)

- For the first time, Abigail relaxes enough to understand that sometimes there is nothing that anyone can do to avert disaster.

    ... not even a mother who had every nerve attuned to anticipate disaster, could have saved [the baby] if the waves leapt up, if life went on as usual and freak accidents peppered a calm shore. (p.223)

SYMBOLS

Counting

Sinkhole

Dark to Light

Snow/Rain

Daffodils

Heaven

SYMBOLS

Counting

Counting is a familiar activity for children and adults alike. In the novel, everyone counts: Mr. Harvey, Ruth, Buckley, Jack Salmon, Susie and Detective Fenerman. Sebold uses this metaphor of counting to account for many things: experiences, bodies, beliefs and disbeliefs.

- Lindsey's friends *"listed the dead they knew."* (p.125)

- Detective Fenerman used the pictures he carried in his wallet to count the unsolved cases on his roster.

- George Harvey counted bones.

   By counting the bones and staying away from the sealed letter, [his mother's wedding ring], the bottle of perfume, he tried to stay away from what he wanted most ... (p.131)

- Abigail counted her children. *"Out loud I said I had two children. Silently, I said three."* (p.281)

- Buckley was full of rage and kept his count *"... daily, weekly, yearly, [in] an underground storage room of hate."* (p.269)

- Susie counted love.

   At some point, to counter the list of the dead, I had begun keeping my own list of the living. (p.271)

   " had always been in love with him. I counted the lashes of each closed eye. (p.283)

   I collected kiss stories. (p.283)

   At twenty-one Lindsey was many things I would never become, but I barely grieved this list anymore. (p.232)

Sinkhole

- Besides being the actual location where Susie was dumped by Harvey, this image represents the process through which certain thoughts take time to sink into our consciousness and how they slowly bubble up to the surface.

- The sinkhole is also a metaphor for grief. Ray asks Ruth, *"How do you know it won't swallow us?"* and Ruth answers, *"We're not heavy enough."* (p.293) When there is too much grief, it can over-

whelm and drown the grieving person. Letting go of grief lightens the burden.

- Ray and Ruth have a mind-altering experience when they watch the sinkhole being filled in.

    > *Ruth was both more tired and more happy than she had ever been. For Ray, what he had been through and the possibilities this opened up for him were just start-ing to sink in.* (p.311)

- As they continue to watch the sinkhole, they see an old gas stove slowly appear. *"Apparently," [Ray] said, "the earth's throat burps."* (p.294) If we accept that things can rise from a sinkhole, then we must consider that there are other hidden things that can suddenly come into view. In this way, it becomes plausible to imagine that we might catch a glimpse of heaven, through a hole in the unseen boundary line between heaven and earth.

Dark to Light

There are images of dark and light throughout the story. Either things take place in the dark, where the emotions of fear and grief match the action, or the characters start from underground and climb to the surface. The goal of reaching the light is to achieve peace, happiness, heaven.

- Susie is murdered in an underground cave built by Mr. Harvey.

- When Susie's death comes to light, her parents react like flowers in nature: *"It was my father who grew toward us as the years went by; it was my mother who grew away."* (p.153)

- When Susie wanders too far from her heaven, it gets dark. (p.120)

- When Ray and Ruth visit the sinkhole, Ray remarks that *"holes in the earth draw on some pretty primal fears."* (p.287)

- Lindsey reaches Harvey's bedroom after breaking into the house through a basement window.

- Lindsey and Samuel enter the Victorian house on a dark, rainy night. As they climb the stairs, they feel like they are climbing out of a cave. This is where Samuel proposes to Lindsey; they have reached the light of their relationship. (p.236, 237)

Snow / Rain

Sebold's use of snow and rain is a traditional literary device, called pathetic fallacy when the description of the weather matches the emotional environment of the plot.

- The story opens in winter, and it is snowing.

- The penguin is trapped in a snow globe, which can also represent the world of death.

- The snow covers the evidence of Susie's murder. Similarly, the emotions of grief are weighed down and buried after the murder.

- Near the end of the story, the snow turns to rain. Lindsey finally is able to cry. Tears are the release of her grief. ("Tears of Heaven", the song)

Daffodils

- Each parent has reacted differently to Susie's death: her father faced the sunlight and grew toward the remaining children; her mother turned away from the light of her living children. (p.153)

- Susie's favorite flower was a bright, sunny daffodil, the first flower of spring. The shape of the daffodil is like an open face. When Susie's father sees the daffodils brought to him in the hospital, he tells Abigail,

  See ... You live in the face of it (Susie's death) by giving her a flower. **(p.280)**

Heaven

- Sebold paints an interesting picture of heaven and bases it partly on the familiar story of The Wizard of Oz. Sebold offers a variation on the theme of Dorothy returning home. Like Dorothy, Susie simply has to understand that home is her heaven and that her earthly home will always remain in her heart and never leave her. *"All you have to do is desire it, and if you desire it enough and understand why ... it will come."* **(p.19)**

- There is no perfect heaven and Sebold does not paint a sugary picture. There is pain on both sides of the veil. Susie has a tough time seeing her father, hovering between life and death, after his heart attack.

  ... die for me/don't die for me ... We stood – the dead child and the living ... both wanting the same thing ... to please us both was an impossibility. **(p.258)**

- Sebold leaves us with a final comforting thought that *"almost everyone in heaven has someone on Earth they watch, a loved one, a friend, or even a stranger who was once kind..."* **(p.246)**

LAST THOUGHTS

A Perfect World

Ruth's Journal

The Novel's End

LAST THOUGHTS

A Perfect World

- For Sebold, there is neither a perfect heaven nor a perfect world, but there is transparency on all sides. Both realms can be shared because life is a snow globe.

- To people on both sides of the veil, the dead should be whatever you want them to be: Susie reassures us that her family *"... would not know when I was gone ... I had become manifest in whatever way they wanted me to become."* (p.301)

- The dead are as individual to each person as is the idea of heaven. There is limited perfection in both images.

Symbols of the Perfect/Imperfect World

- **Transparent worlds:** Sebold uses the images of the snow globe and the ship in the bottle to illustrate her idea of parallel worlds, or a world within a world. These worlds can co-exist and not contradict each other. She presents both a positive and negative way of looking out from or looking in at life. One idea of negative transparency is shown as a frozen image under ice; another example is Susie's description of her parents frozen in grief. (p.290)

- **Non-transparent worlds:** The symbols Sebold uses to show non-transparency are Harvey's tent, Buckley's fort, and the underground cave. In these places, one can't see out or in; in this way, these symbols represent viewpoints that are limited or closed. These symbols also imitate or pretend to be others. For example, Buckley's tent parallels Harvey's marriage tent; the underground cave is stocked like a hideaway play fort.

- **Captured worlds:** Sebold uses the symbol of the photograph in the same way she uses the symbol of ice.

    - *The photo Susie takes of her mother captures a glimpse of her mother's unborn wishes. Each wish later becomes a living child, but this was not her initial life's goal. Not only does she not get her wish to be a free and independent spirit, now she no longer even has her child. Susie's death begins the process of the destruction of Abigail's most secret desires and recovery.*

    - *The photo Susie takes of her father shows his face filling a three-by-three square. In order to see it properly, the photo must be turned on a forty-five-degree angle so that it appears as a diamond shape. This makes the image of her dad special. It is like heaven, which is also special, and which must be turned in order to be viewed from a different angle.* (p.239)

Ruth's Journal

Ruth's journal is this novel.

> *Ruth ... was still trying to find a way to write down whom she saw and what she had experienced. Ruth ... wanted everyone to believe what she knew: that the dead truly talk to us, that in the air between the living, spirits bob and weave and laugh with us. They are the oxygen we breathe.* (p.325)

- In order to accept this premise, it is necessary to further explore the ideas of possibility and plausibility. (see Structure, p.37) Sebold works with the thought that what is possible can more easily be disproved and dismissed. It is more difficult to reject what is plausible: an unsolved murder is possible, but may not be able to be proved; an icicle murder is plausible and can be understood using logic and faith. No other proof is necessary.

- If we can accept the difference between these two ideas, then we move onto Sebold's other, more difficult example.

    ○ The reality of Susie entering Ruth's body and making love to Ray may not be possible, but it may be plausible. It may be more easily imagined that Ray, in fact, fantasized the love scene between himself and Susie after reading Ruth's journal. He opens himself to this possibility and allows himself to dream of it.

    ○ Susie validates the possibility of this thought: *"I saw how hope was what I had traded on in heaven and on Earth. Dreams of being a wildlife photographer ... dreams of kissing Ray Singh once more. Look what happens when you dream."* (p.310)

This is the main confirming thought of the novel.

The Novel's End

> *I wish you all a long and happy life.* **(p.328)**

- In a lesser novel, this last sentence might have spoiled the entire read. In this novel, this ending opens up many new thoughts.

- This final statement is the "letting go" that both Sebold and Susie talk about. It is simultaneously a sign-off and a wish for good things to come.

- As a signature greeting from Susie, this declaration fits with Susie's adolescent personality as we come to know it. The novel's opening could be the start of a letter or a diary entry. Susie's informal, conversational tone is reminiscent of Anne Frank's diary.

- This novel is a special letter to all of Sebold's readers. Because her personal story is well known and well documented, Sebold reassures us that she is all right. In her open and generous way, Susie wants us to also benefit from her story. She uses Ruth to do it.

> *[Ruth] would always feel me and think of me ... All of it, the story of my life and death, was hers if she chose to tell it ...* **(p.321)**

And now it's done.

FROM THE NOVEL

FROM THE NOVEL ...

Memorable quotes from the Text of

The Lovely Bones

PAGE 6. ... on December 6, 1973, it was snowing, and I took a shortcut through the cornfield back from the junior high.

PAGE 8. I was in my heaven by that time, fitting my limbs together, and couldn't believe his (Harvey's) audacity. "That man has no shame," I said to Franny, my intake counselor. "Exactly," she said, and made her point as simply as that. There wasn't a lot of bullshit in my heaven.

PAGE 36. The odd thing about Earth was what we saw when we looked down. Besides the initial view that you might suspect, the old ants-from-the-skyscraper phenomenon, there were souls leaving bodies all over the world.

notes

PAGE 43. Holiday [the dog] ... was watching my mother. She had a stare that stretched to infinity. She was, in that moment, not my mother but something separate from me... [her eyes] were bottomless in a way that I found frightening. I had an instinct then ... [that] I should take a photograph with my new camera."

PAGE 78. After the cornfield was roped off, searched, then abandoned, Ruth went walking there. She would wrap a large wool shawl of her grandmother's around her under the ratty old peacoat of her father's. Soon she noted that teachers ... were happy not to have her there: her intelligence made her a problem.

PAGE 79. [Ruth] talked to herself, and sometimes she thought about me. Often she would rest a moment against the chain-link fence that separated the soccer field from the track, while she watched the world come alive around her ...

I grew to love Ruth on those mornings, feeling that in some way we could never explain on our opposite sides of the Inbetween, we were born to keep each other company. Odd girls who had found each other in the strangest way – in the shiver she had felt when I passed.

PAGE 90. "Do you see her?" Buckley asked Nate as they climbed the stairs ... "That's my sister."'

... I had never even let myself yearn for Buckley, afraid he might see my image in a mirror or a bottle cap. Like everyone else I was trying to protect him. "Too young," I said to Franny. "Where do you think imaginary friends come from?" she said.

PAGE 111, 112. Ray Singh stayed away. He said goodbye to me in his own way: by looking at a picture ... that I had given him that fall ...

What did dead mean, Ray wondered. It meant lost, it meant frozen, it meant gone. He knew that no one ever really looked the way they did in photos. He knew he didn't look as wild or as frightened as he did in his

own. He came to realize something as he stared at my photo – that it was not me. I was in the air around him ... I was the girl he had chosen to kiss. He wanted, somehow, to set me free.

PAGE 119, 120. [Susie] If I walked too far and wondered loud enough the fields would change ...and I could hear it then – singing – a kind of low humming and moaning warning me back from the edge. My head would throb and the sky would darken... that perpetual yesterday lived again ... I came up to the lip of my grave this way many times but had yet to stare in.

... I did begin to wonder what the word heaven meant ...

[Franny tells her] "You have to stop desiring certain answers"...

... stop asking why you were killed instead of someone else, stop investigating the vacuum left by your loss, stop wondering what everyone left on Earth is feeling ... Simply put, you have to give up on Earth.

PAGE 140. I stood in the room beside him and watched him sleep. During the night the story had come unwound and spun down so that the police understood: Mr. Salmon was crazy with grief and had gone out to the corn-field seeking revenge. It fit what they knew of him, his persistent phone calls, his obsession with the neighbor, and Detective Fenerman having visited that same day to tell my parents that for all intents and purposes my murder investigation had entered a sort of hiatus. No clues were left to pursue. No body had been found.

PAGE 145. "When the dead are done with the living," Franny said to me, "the living can go on to other things."

"What about the dead?" I asked. "Where do we go?"

She wouldn't answer me."

PAGE 154. I had played a hide-and-seek game of love with my mother as I grew up, courting her attention and approval in a way that I had never had to with my father.

I didn't have to play ... anymore ... As she stood in the darkened room and watched my sister and father, I knew one of the things that heaven meant. I had a choice, and it was not to divide my family in my heart.

PAGE 159, 160. ... [Jack] had set his return to work for December 2, right after Thanksgiving. He wanted to be back in the office by the anniversary of my disappearance. Functioning and catching up on work – in as public and distracting a place as he could think of. And away from my mother, if he was honest with himself.

... all her energy was against the house, and all his energy was inside it.

PAGE 216. When my brother turned seven, he built a fort for me. It was something the two of us had said we would always do together and something that my father could not bring himself to do. It reminded him too much of building the tent with the disappeared Mr. Harvey.

A family with five little girls had moved into Mr. Harvey's house. Laughter traveled over into my father's study ... The sound of little girls – girls to spare.

PAGE 226, 227. [Ruth] had become convinced that she had a second sight that no one else had. She didn't know what to do with it, save taking copious notes for the future, but she had grown unafraid. The world she saw of dead women and children had become as real to her as the world in which she lived.

PAGE 230, 231. Years passed ... I watched my family and my friends and neighbors ... But I would end each day with my father in his den.

I would lay these photographs down in my mind, those gathered from my constant watching, and I could trace how one thing – my death – connected these images to a single source. No one could have predicted how my loss would change small moments on Earth. But I held on to those moments, hoarded them. None of them were lost as long as I was watching.

PAGE 270. "My girl," [Jack] breathed out heavily.

... "Look what it took to get you home."

... To see them together was like a tenuous belief made real.

My father could see glimmers, like the colored flecks inside my mother's eyes – things to hold on to."

PAGE 287, 288. ... Joe Ellis had never recovered from being accused of killing the cats and dogs Mr. Harvey had killed. He wandered around ... wanting so much to take solace in the love of cats and dogs. For me the saddest thing was that these animals smelled the brokenness in him – the human defect – and kept away.

PAGE 296, 297. I could see Mr. Harvey take the turn into my old neighborhood in broad daylight, past caring who spotted him, even depending on his standard invisibility ...

He drove down the road a few houses further.

There she was, my precious sister ...

It was then that I began to see them coming down the road.

... I saw the final vestiges of the animals and the women taking leave of Mr. Harvey's house. They straggled forward together. He watched my sister and thought of the sheets he had draped on the poles of the bridal tent. He had stared right in my father's eyes that day as he said my name.

PAGE 303, 304. He kissed me lightly again, on the lips ... The brush of his lips, the slight stubble of his beard as it grazed me, and the sound of the kiss ... then the more brutal breaking away. It reverberated, this sound, down the long tunnel of loneliness and making do with watching the touch and caress of others on Earth. I had never been touched like this. I had only been hurt by hands past all tenderness. But spreading out into my heaven after death had been a moonbeam that swirled and blinked on and off – Ray Singh's kiss. Somehow Ruth knew this.

notes

PAGE 304. "Where do you want to go?" Ray asked.

And it was such a wide question, the answer so vast. I knew I did not want to chase after Mr. Harvey. I looked at Ray and knew why I was there. To take back a piece of heaven I had never known.

ACKNOWLEDGEMENTS

ACKNOWLEDGEMENTS

Backer, B., Hannon, R., & Russell, N. (1994). *Death & Dying: Understanding & Care*, 2nd Ed. Delmar Publishing, Albany, N.Y. 2003.

Barnes & Noble. *Alice Sebold Biography*. www.barnesandnoble.com

Berry, Michelle. "Simply Heavenly". *The Globe and Mail*. Toronto, July 13, 2002.

Press, Joy. "Heaven Can't Wait". *The Village Voice*, New York. June, 2002.

Rowe, Georgia, "Bones. Success Surprises Sebold". *New York Times*, Sunday, August 4, 2002. (posted article)